Julian

by

DAYAL KAUR KHALSA

Tundra Books

I once lived in a little house in the country with two gentle cats: Victoria, who was named Victoria because she was born on Queen Victoria's birthday, and her kitten, Ricky Rainbow, who was named Ricky Rainbow because on the day he was born there was a rainbow in the sky. We lived together very peacefully.

There was one problem, though. The vegetable garden was rapidly being nibbled down by groundhogs.

Our neighbor, Bob, who had a farm down the road, said, "What you need is a good barking dog to chase the groundhogs away." Since I had always wanted a dog, that seemed like a fine solution. "I know just the dog for you," he added. "He's a real good chaser."

A few days later Bob drove up, but before he could even open the door of his truck, a huge yellow dog jumped out of the window and ran barking after the cats.

Victoria and Ricky Rainbow scrambled up on top of the fence posts to safety.

Bob said the dog's name was Julian.

Well, Julian certainly was a good chaser.
He chased the cows in the next pasture.

He chased my car down the bumpy road.
 He even chased the groundhogs out of the garden.
 And he chased and he chased and he chased the cats all over
the place. They didn't like Julian at all.

There was one animal, though, who actually *enjoyed* being chased by Julian. She was Bob's racehorse, Josie.

But there was one animal Julian could *not* chase—Bob's pet goat, Billy. Every morning Billy would jump up on the seat of Bob's motorcycle and stand there all day. He'd lower his head and try to butt anyone who came near. Even Julian.

Julian didn't chase me either, but he was always barking at me and jumping up on me—especially when I went down to the well for water. He liked to try to knock the bucket out of my hand.

One afternoon as I was kneeling down dipping water from the well, Julian jumped up on me so hard I fell over backward—and he went bounding headfirst right down into the well. He made a tremendous splash.

At first I thought, "It serves you right." But then I saw that Julian couldn't get out. He was paddling around in a little circle, barking frantically for help.

I tried to pull him out, but every time I grabbed his paws, he would jerk away from me. He was such a big dog I was afraid he might drag me right down into the well with him.

We were both getting very tired. Julian's big bark had dwindled into a sad little whimper. Finally, I lay down on my stomach so I could get a firmer hold on him. I grabbed his paws and pulled with all my might. Julian pushed off from the side of the well—and he came flying out.

When we got back to the house, I had a little talk with Julian.

I explained to him that I didn't like the way he behaved. It was true, he was doing a good job of keeping the groundhogs out of the garden. But I didn't like him jumping on me and always chasing the cats. And I wished he would just cut it out so we could all live in peace together.

I don't know how much of that conversation Julian understood, or whether it was just that he was grateful to me for getting him out of the well. But whatever the reason, Julian never barked at me or jumped all over me again.

In fact, he became as good a dog as anyone could ever want. He was my loyal friend. He went with me everywhere.

Our favorite outing was to drive around the back country roads at sunset, listening to country music blaring on the radio.

Not that Julian still didn't have his quirks . . .

He liked to sleep stretched out on the couch. And he snored in his sleep.

Whenever I tried to play Frisbee with him, he'd run away and bury it.

And if I left him in the car by himself, well . . . One day, when we were out driving, I stopped off for a donut and a cup of tea. I left Julian in the car.

As I was sitting at the counter, the man next to me said, "Hey, lady, I think there's something wrong with your car. The stop lights keep blinking on and off."

I went out to see what was the matter.

There was Julian, crouched down on the floor, pumping the brake pedal with his great big paw. He didn't like being left all alone in the car. After that, I always got my order *to go*.

And, of course, he still chased Victoria and Ricky Rainbow. No matter where they were, he'd sniff them out—and go barking off after them.

Those cats were always having to climb on top of furniture and fence posts and trees out of Julian's reach. I was almost afraid Ricky Rainbow might grow up thinking he was a bird instead of a cat—he spent so much time perching.

ne evening as I was sitting in the kitchen with Julian, Victoria rushed into the house. She darted all over the kitchen, then ran into the parlor, searched under the couch and up on the shelves. She came back into the kitchen, meowing loudly. She sounded very, very upset.

I couldn't imagine what was bothering her. Her bowl was full of milk, and, for once, Julian wasn't chasing her or Ricky Rainbow. But—where *was* Ricky Rainbow? Then I realized what was the matter. Ricky Rainbow was missing!

"Julian," I said, "you can finally use that big nose of yours to do something good. Go find Ricky Rainbow!"

Julian shot out the door and sniffed hard. He quickly picked up the scent of Ricky Rainbow and raced down the lane. Victoria was right behind him. He headed straight to the tall birch tree at the bottom of the hill.

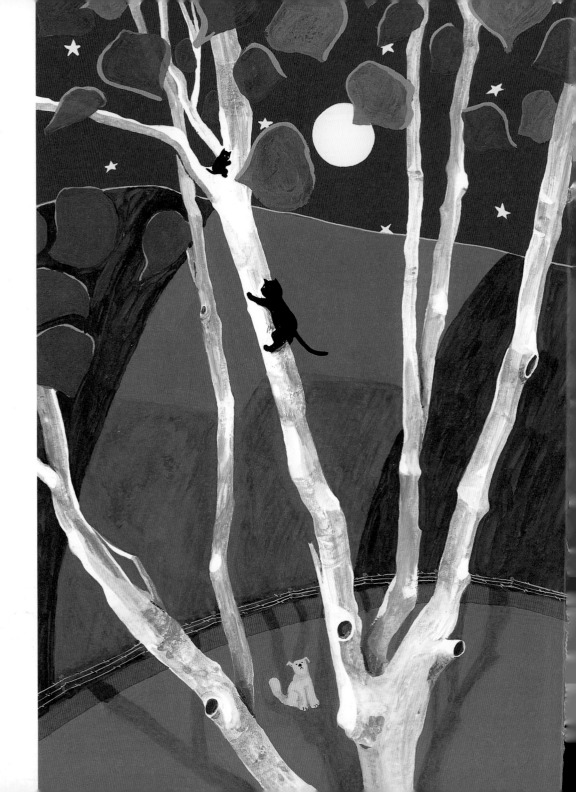

Way up, huddled on a branch, sat little Ricky Rainbow. He had wandered off exploring and climbed up the big tree. But he didn't know how to get down.

Victoria raced up the tree, picked him up by the scruff of his neck, and brought him safely to the ground. Then we all went back home and had a party to celebrate Ricky Rainbow's rescue.

After that night things were very different around our house.

Julian looked after those cats as if they were his little sister and brother.

And to Victoria and Ricky Rainbow, Julian was a great hero.

He never chased the cats again.

Instead, they were the best of friends. Every morning they all came with me while I did the chores.

And every afternoon we took a long, brisk walk in the woods together.

And every night after supper, while I read or watched the fire slowly die down, Julian would stretch out on the couch, Ricky Rainbow asleep next to his nose and Victoria curled up in his tail—a happy, peaceful, little family.

For Yogi Bhajan
and all his children

Published in Canada by Tundra Books,
Montreal, Quebec   H3G 1R4

Published in the United States by
Clarkson N. Potter, Inc.

Manufactured in Japan

Design by Jan Melchior

Canadian Cataloguing in Publication Data

Khalsa, Dayal Kaur, 1943–
Julian
Summary: Julian, a high-spirited farm dog,
makes life very uncomfortable for the house cat,
Victoria, until he helps save her lost kitten.
1. Dogs—Juvenile fiction.   I. Title.
PS8571.H35J84 1989   jC813'.54
PZ10.3.K43Ju 1989   C89-090150-3

ISBN 0-88776-237-9

10 9 8 7 6 5 4 3 2 1

First Canadian Edition